TOUSSAINT L'OUVERTURE

The Fight for Haiti's Freedom

TOUSSAINT L'OUVERTURE

The Fight for Haiti's Freedom

Paintings by **Jacob Lawrence**

Written by **Walter Dean Myers**

Simon & Schuster Books for Young Readers

SIMON & SCHUSTER BOOKS FOR YOUNG READERS

An imprint of Simon & Schuster Children's Publishing Division

1230 Avenue of the Americas, New York, New York 10020

SIMON & SCHUSTER BOOKS FOR YOUNG READERS is a trademark of Simon & Schuster.

The text for this book is set in Aldus Roman.

Printed and bound in the United States of America

First Edition

10 9 8 7 6 5 4 3 2 1

Library of Congress Cataloging-in-Publication Data

Myers, Walter Dean, 1937—

Toussaint L'Ouverture : the fight for Haiti's freedom / paintings by Jacob Lawrence ;

written by Walter Dean Myers   p.   cm.

Summary: A collection of paintings by Jacob Lawrence chronicling the liberation of

Haiti in 1804 under the leadership of General Toussaint L'Ouverture.

ISBN 0-689-80126-2

1. Toussaint L'Ouverture, 1743?-1803—Juvenile literature. 2. Toussaint L'Ouverture, 1743?-

1803— Portraits. 3. Haiti—History—Revolution, 1791-1804—Juvenile literature. 4. Haiti—

History—Revolution, 1791-1804—Pictorial works. [1. Toussaint L'Ouverture, 1743?-1803.

2. Haiti—History—Revolution, 1791-1804.] I. Lawrence, Jacob, 1917— ill. II. Title.

F1923.T69M94 1996 972.94'03'092—dc20 95-30046

My family arrived in New York's Harlem community in 1930 when I was thirteen years of age. It was during the Great Depression. During my frequent meanderings through the streets of Harlem, I would hear the many street orators tell of the deeds and exploits of black people such as Frederick Douglass, Marcus Garvey, Harriet Tubman, Nat Turner, Denmark Vesey, and Toussaint L'Ouverture, who liberated the slaves of Haiti.

These orators would tell their stories with pride, drama, and great passion, and I would listen in awe and excitement. These were heroes to whom I could relate. I was inspired and motivated to tell these stories in paint—in a serious form. My first subject was Toussaint L'Ouverture, a very brave and brilliant leader who defeated those who would enslave him, and in so doing, deny him and others equality, justice, and fraternity.

In winning the battle for Haiti's freedom, Toussaint L'Ouverture joined the ranks of those who have fought and contributed much to our continuous struggle for liberty.

Toussaint L'Ouverture was a great man. He will always remain one of my heroes.

Jacob Lawrence
Seattle, Washington
October 1996

Toussaint L'Ouverture had seen his people suffer under the Spanish and French rulers of Hispaniola, the second largest island in the West Indies. He had seen them cruelly beaten and their dreams of freedom crushed on the plantations on which they worked as slaves. But it was Toussaint, with genius and determination, who would lead his people in their struggle for freedom and break the chains of bondage.

On December 6, 1492, on his first trip to the New World, Christopher Columbus planted the Spanish flag on an island he called Hispaniola, or "Little Spain." The people who lived on the island called their land Haiti, the Land of Mountains.

The Spanish searched for gold, forcing the Taino and Carib Indians who lived on the island to work long hours. Killed if they refused to work and suffering from diseases brought to the island by the Spanish, the Indian population dropped to a few thousand.

The French also wanted the rich island and a bitter struggle between the two powerful nations, Spain and France, lasted for years.

By 1691, two hundred years after Columbus first landed on Hispaniola, the two nations had decided to divide the country between them. Spain called its part Santo Domingo, and France called its section Saint Domingue.

Captured Africans were brought to Saint Domingue to work as slaves when the Indian population had been wiped out. Their treatment was just as brutal.

On the twentieth of May, 1743, Francois Dominique Toussaint was born. His mother worked on the Breda plantation. His father, an African educated by the Jesuits, taught young Toussaint to read and speak French.

As a child, Toussaint heard the awful sound of the planter's whip and saw blood stream from the bodies of black men and women.

There were no schools for blacks, but Toussaint taught himself by reading all the books he could find. During this time he worked as a coachman on the Breda plantation.

As Toussaint grew to manhood he learned of two exciting events. The first was the American Revolution, which had begun in 1776. The second was the overthrow of the French monarchy in 1789. Toussaint dreamed of a day when he, too, would be free.

Wealthy white plantation owners ruled Saint Domingue.
They considered themselves superior to people of mixed races,
but they were especially cruel to the enslaved Africans.

In England and France there were societies that fought for the rights of those enslaved. Toussaint read books that celebrated freedom, and the dignity of all men. He came to believe in the idea of freedom as a basic human right and that if violence was needed to overthrow slavery, then he could not turn away from it.

On the twenty-second of August, 1791, the blacks rebelled against the plantation owners. Racing through the night they began to set fire to the plantations, killing many of those who held them in slavery.

Toussaint, desperately yearning for his own freedom, was still a kindly man. Moved by his feelings toward them, he led his master and mistress to safety.

Hundreds, then thousands of blacks bound by slavery joined the rebellion. Toussaint joined the uprising and soon demonstrated his ability at organizing his soldiers and planning battles.

Many of the mulattoes, those of mixed race, had never been
slaves. They only wanted equality with whites. Sometimes they
sided with the black rebels, and at other times they fought
alongside the whites.

Toussaint's small force began to win battle after battle.

In a fierce battle against the French, Toussaint forced an opening in their ranks to gain a victory. After that battle he took the name L'Ouverture, which means "the opener."

Toussaint's well-organized fighters were a match for even the highly trained French soldiers.

Angry blacks often slaughtered those who still wished to enslave them.

Spanish soldiers arrived, hoping for an opportunity to regain land from the French. British slaveholders were afraid that if the blacks won in Saint Domingue, the uprising would spread to the British West Indies. British soldiers arrived to help defeat the blacks. Toussaint L'Ouverture faced them all with courage.

Toussaint moved his army swiftly about the island.

He planned carefully, never risking more than he should, and never putting his army in a dangerous position.

His soldiers learned to love and respect Toussaint both as a man and as a general.

Toussaint understood and respected the abilities of those who fought with him, and used those abilities well.

The world was aware of his victories, and wondered what effect they would have on slavery in places like the United States.

Here was a man who had taken black workers from the
plantations and formed them into a mighty army of liberation.

Toussaint L'Ouverture controlled most of Saint Domingue by 1800. He began to make plans to strengthen the economy of the country.

Toussaint had a new constitution prepared.

He then turned his attention to Santo Domingo, the other
part of the island of Hispaniola. Leading a large, well-disciplined
army, Toussaint soon defeated the Spanish of Santo Domingo.
He quickly abolished slavery there, as well.

But on the other side of the ocean there was another man wishing to strengthen his country's economy. That man was Napoléon Bonaparte. One way to add to the wealth of France was to regain control of Saint Domingue, and to bring back slavery.

Napoléon sent a fleet of ships and troops, under General Charles Leclerc, to defeat Toussaint.

The sheer size of this invading French army meant trouble
for Toussaint.

The French fought well on flat ground, so Toussaint took his
men into the mountains. He would make the French come to
him and fight on his terms.

The French won victories against the black soldiers, but they were costly ones in which hundreds of French soldiers died. Leclerc began to negotiate with Toussaint and offered to make him lieutenant governor of Saint Domingue if he stopped fighting. Toussaint understood Leclerc's true intent. He continued the struggle.

French troops were dying in battle and from disease. It was also hard for the French to get supplies to their men. Leclerc wanted to negotiate with Toussaint.

Toussaint understood that if the French sent more troops, and he was sure they would, he could not defeat them. Painfully, he agreed to end the fighting. The French commander guaranteed the freedom of the blacks, and promised to take black officers into the French army. But when Toussaint laid down his arms he was immediately taken prisoner. Leclerc had lied. It was the seventh of June, 1802.

In France, the dungeon of the Castle Joux was dark and cold.
It was a crushing blow to the man who so loved his freedom.

It became clear that Napoléon intended to restore slavery in Saint Domingue. For the blacks it was a clear choice—fight as free people, or live as slaves. Black men, women, and children took up arms in a desperate struggle to preserve their freedom.

Toussaint would not live to see his beloved country gain its final independence. In April 1803, far away from his homeland, Toussaint L'Ouverture died in his desolate cell.

But the struggle that Toussaint L'Ouverture had begun was finally triumphant. In November 1803 the French ended their attempts to defeat the people of this small island. The new leaders signed a declaration of independence on January 1, 1804, for the country they now called Haiti.

Jean-Jacques Dessalines, who had been part of the fight for freedom, was the leader of the new Republic of Haiti. But the spirit of Toussaint L'Ouverture lived on in Haiti. In the quest for freedom the people of Haiti had won. The chains of slavery had been broken.

The Toussaint L'Ouverture Series and The Amistad Research Center

The Haitians, along with the American colonies and France herself, were pioneers in the modern wars of liberation. Thus the Haitian rebellion, and Toussaint himself in particular, would always have a special symbolic role for people of color around the world. This was certainly the case for an African-American art student in Harlem during the late 1930s. Not yet twenty-one, Lawrence was part of a new wave of black expression in painting that was just then appearing from the brushes of Romare Bearden, William H. Johnson, Archibald Motley, and others. Lawrence sought a way to express his own revolutionary artistic identity and provide social commentary on the Jim Crow laws and racism of his time. The story of Toussaint provided his inspiration but proved to be a tale too big for a single frame. Instead, Lawrence invented a broad narrative style and told his story on forty-one different panels. He surrounded himself with canvases—laying on the colors one at a time to produce the singular tale presented in this book.

The Toussaint L'Ouverture series also launched Lawrence's career. Today Jacob Lawrence is recognized as a treasure, both in America and abroad. Mr. Lawrence has twelve honorary doctorates and a list of other awards, ranging from the National Medal of Arts to the Spingarn Medal of the NAACP. The Amistad Research Center is proud to hold the entire Toussaint L'Ouverture series, which forms the pictorial basis for this text. The Center is also delighted to work with Mr. Lawrence in developing an ongoing set of limited-edition signed serigraphs for collectors of fine art.

The Amistad Research Center is itself named after a successful and equally stirring revolt—one that took place on the Spanish slave ship *La Amistad* in 1839. With more than 10 million documents, the Center has emerged as the nation's largest independent African-American archives. Amistad also holds one of the country's finest African-American art collections, including Ellis Wilson's *The Funeral Procession*. The Amistad Research Center invites participation in helping to collect and preserve African-American history. The Center is located on the campus of Tulane University in New Orleans, and can also be reached on the World Wide Web site, at http://www.arc.tulane.edu.

Dr. Frederick J. Stielow
The Amistad Research Center
6823 St. Charles Avenue
New Orleans, Louisiana 70118